Now I Wish Upon A Pearl

The Story of Adaline the Mermaid and Suzanne the Girl Growing Up Along Florida's Emerald Coast

Written and illustrated by Marjorie Schoelles, Artistic Entrepreneur

"guaranteed to create **smiles, hugs** and a bit of **magic** for **young girls**, and girls **young at heart**"

Special Thanks:

To Adaline and Suzanne for inspiring the mermaid and girl in this book.

My husband, Tony Grossman, who provides unconditional love and support in my creative endeavours, including sitting inside doing research on a beautiful fall day. And for the gift he brought to our marriage of three phenomenal young adults, Sam, Evan and Suzanne.

My sisters Dianne and Joni, brother Chris and extended family members Jerry and Dave for giving me a reason to think bigger.

For my parents, Orin and Christine Schoelles and their great love of the Gulf Coast. And my Aunt Pearl who would always listen to a young girls dreams. Mom, Daddy and Aunt Pearl are no longer with us but I know they are so very proud and pleased with the message of hope and goodness we are sharing.

For my other parents gifted to me when I married Tony; Mary Ellen and Leonard Grossman and the whole Grossman/Doll clan - thank you for welcoming me so warmly in to the family.

Kenneth and Virginia Tucker who would scoop me up on the weekends for adventures and taught me how to swim.

Thank you to Emmett Smelser for his wonderful editing and the years of encouragment and support.

My circle of trusted friends, Paul Vargas, being my Best Bud always, Kathy Davis as my honorary sister, John H Curry and Steve Gordon for the unshakable belief in my talents and the support through these last years of challenges and Deanna Mims for being the first and best fan of Mermaid Sand.

And finally, the ability to bring an idea to fruition and make it bigger, bolder and market ready would not have been possible without the influence of the people and organization of Glazer-Kennedy Insiders Circle. If I thought I dreamed big before it is nothing compared to dreaming and implementing now. Thank you Dan Kennedy.

And finally, the ability to find my niche and focus our resources owe a great deal to Ryan Deiss and his team. Thank you!

2013 by Marjorie Schoelles, Mermaid Sand ™
All Rights Reserved ISBN 987-0-9846588-0-0

Illustrations and cover design: Marjorie Schoelles Printed in the United States of America

First Edition, Hardcover

To Sophie & Elanor,

Just like Adaline & Suzanne you each have true gifts. Creativity, imagination and so much more!

All the best!
Marjorie 2/18

And now the story begins...

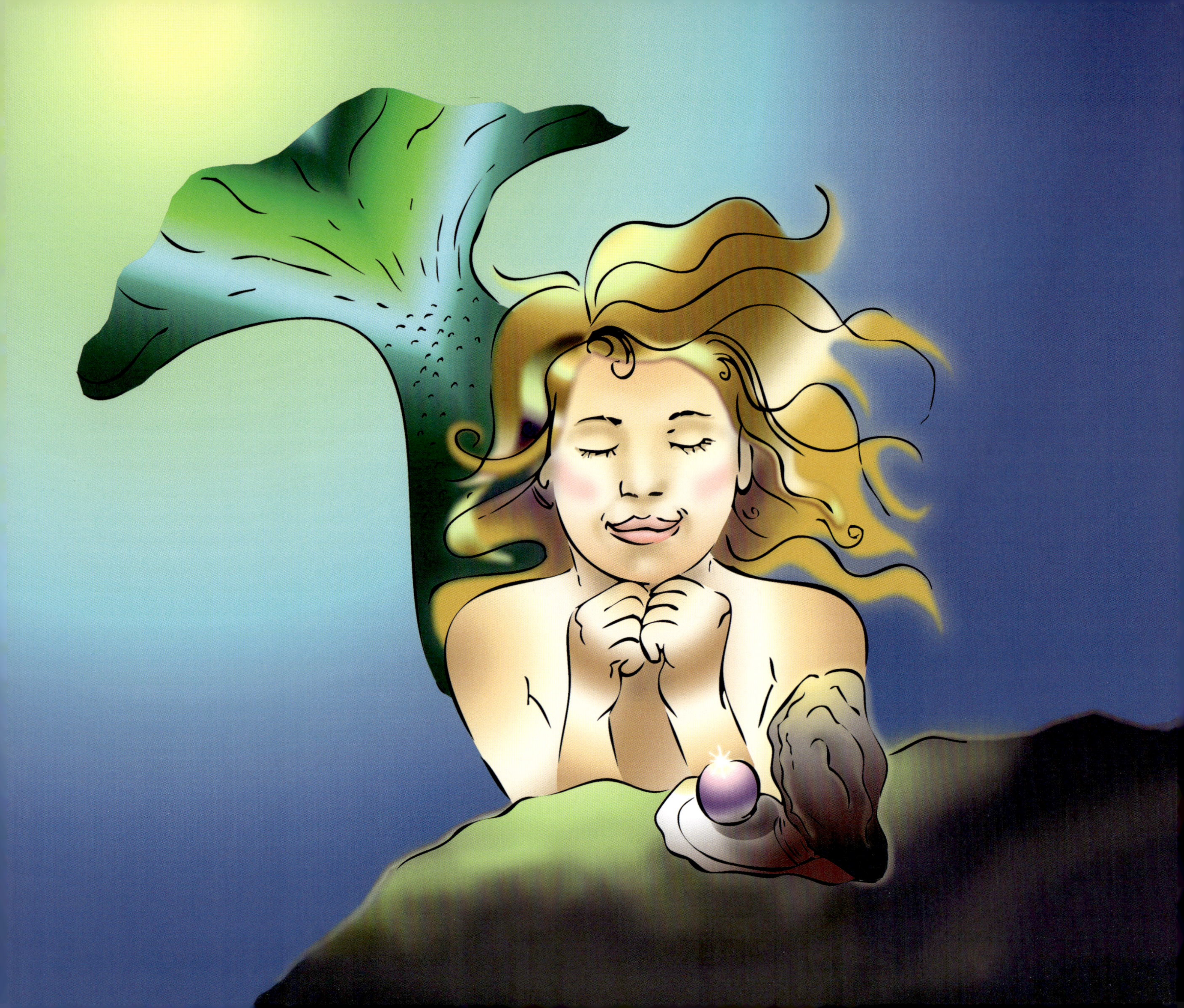

Adaline lives along the Emerald Coast, in Florida waters clean and clear. Being a young mermaid she is drawn to the beauty of shorelines and the wonders of nature outside her natural home.

One day, while playing under the watchful eyes of dolphins in the waters near shore, Adaline saw a wondrous creature…looking much the same age, but different. The young creature was moving, what Adaline had heard of as running, chasing a smaller creature from dune to water's edge.

When Adaline swam back home with questions, her mer-parents quietly smiled and explained she had seen a human girl, playing with a puppy – that both would grow over time, the puppy quickly to a loyal dog, the girl similar to Adaline.

The idea of a girl, on two legs, able to run at will upon the land, was fascinating to Adaline. And though she was a generous young mermaid at heart, she felt a bit of envy for the other girl, able to freely explore the beach and beyond.

Pondering this new discovery, Adaline swam to the entrance of her secret cave, opening the special oyster from Apalachicola Bay her father had told her held a magical "wishing pearl." As the hidden pearl glowed in a shaft of light from above, Adaline clasped her hands under her chin, closed her eyes and began:

"Now I wish upon a pearl, to be a different kind of girl, one that runs wild and free, chasing a puppy from dune to sea."

Being a girl who loved the outdoors, Suzanne knew she was lucky to live in the small town of Mexico Beach. Located along Florida's Emerald Coast, the sugar sand beaches and clear waters were a sight to see. Being so close to the beach meant Suzanne could take her new Labrador puppy, Kelly, to run along the shore every day.

One day, as they were playing fetch in the sand, Suzanne caught a glimmer of movement from the water. She was delighted, but not surprised, to see dolphins playing in the waves between the shore and sandbar.

What did surprise her was a glimpse of blond tresses and a sparkling green fin or tail.
Confused by what she had seen, Suzanne sought out her grandmother, a woman both wise and knowing about nature along the coast.

Without hesitation her grandmother smiled a knowing smile and reassured her that all was well. From the description, Suzanne's grandmother surmised she had seen a young mermaid, as their colors get brighter in hair and tail as they mature. "Suzanne, my dear, you have seen a young mermaid with her dolphin friends. Mermaids are shy creatures, able to swim great distances, often fascinated with the happenings beyond their underwater world"

Being a generous and kind young girl Suzanne hugged her grandmother and thanked her for sharing her knowledge. But in the deepest part of her heart, there was a small bit of envy for that young mermaid able to swim wild and free.

Pondering this new discovery, Suzanne walked to her favorite dune, carrying a "magical wishing pearl" her grandmother had brought her from a special oyster bed in Apalachicola Bay. Sitting upon the sand, the pearl cradled in her hands, eyes closed, she began:

"Now I wish upon a pearl, to be a different kind of girl, one that swims wild and free, playing with dolphins undersea."

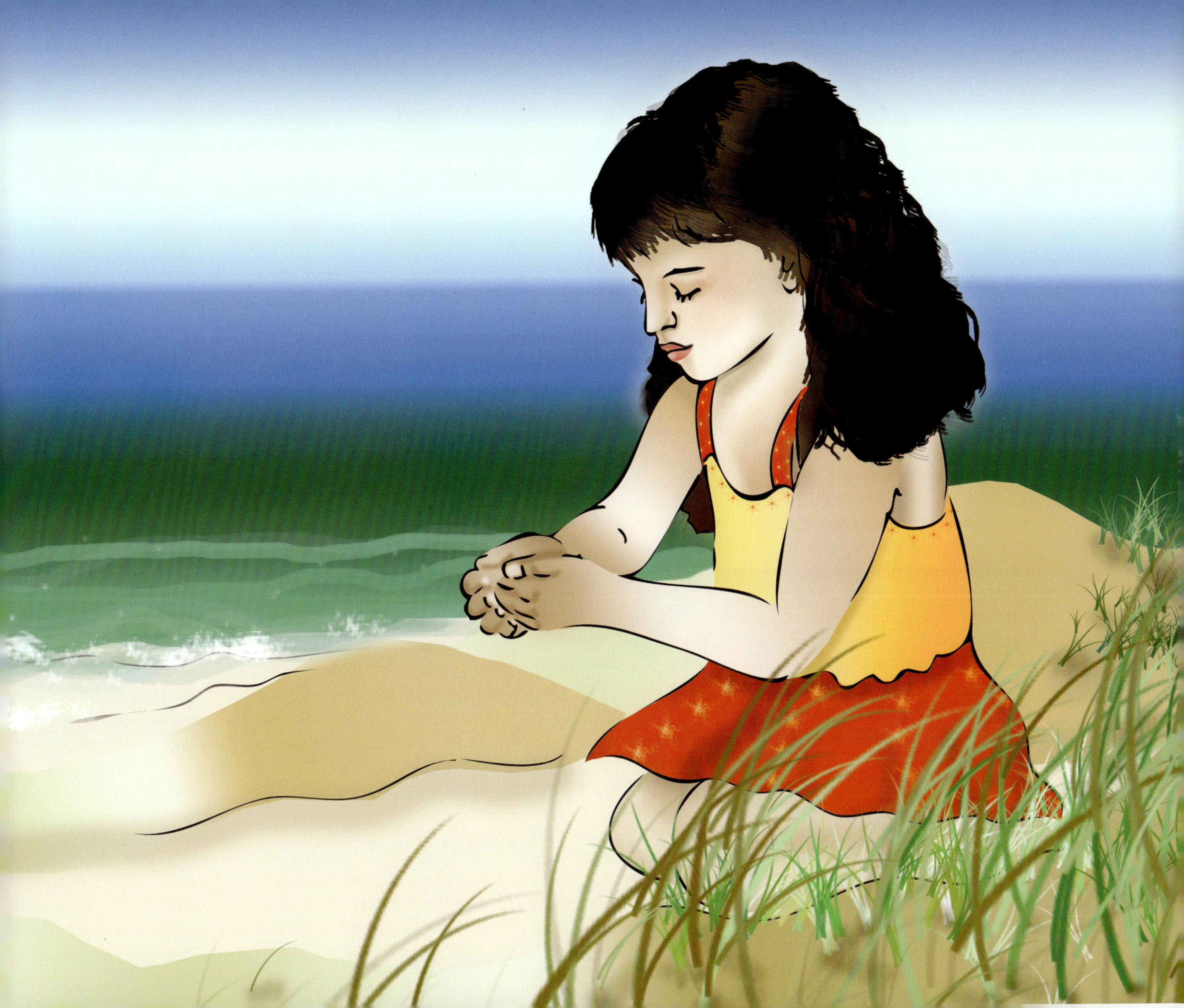

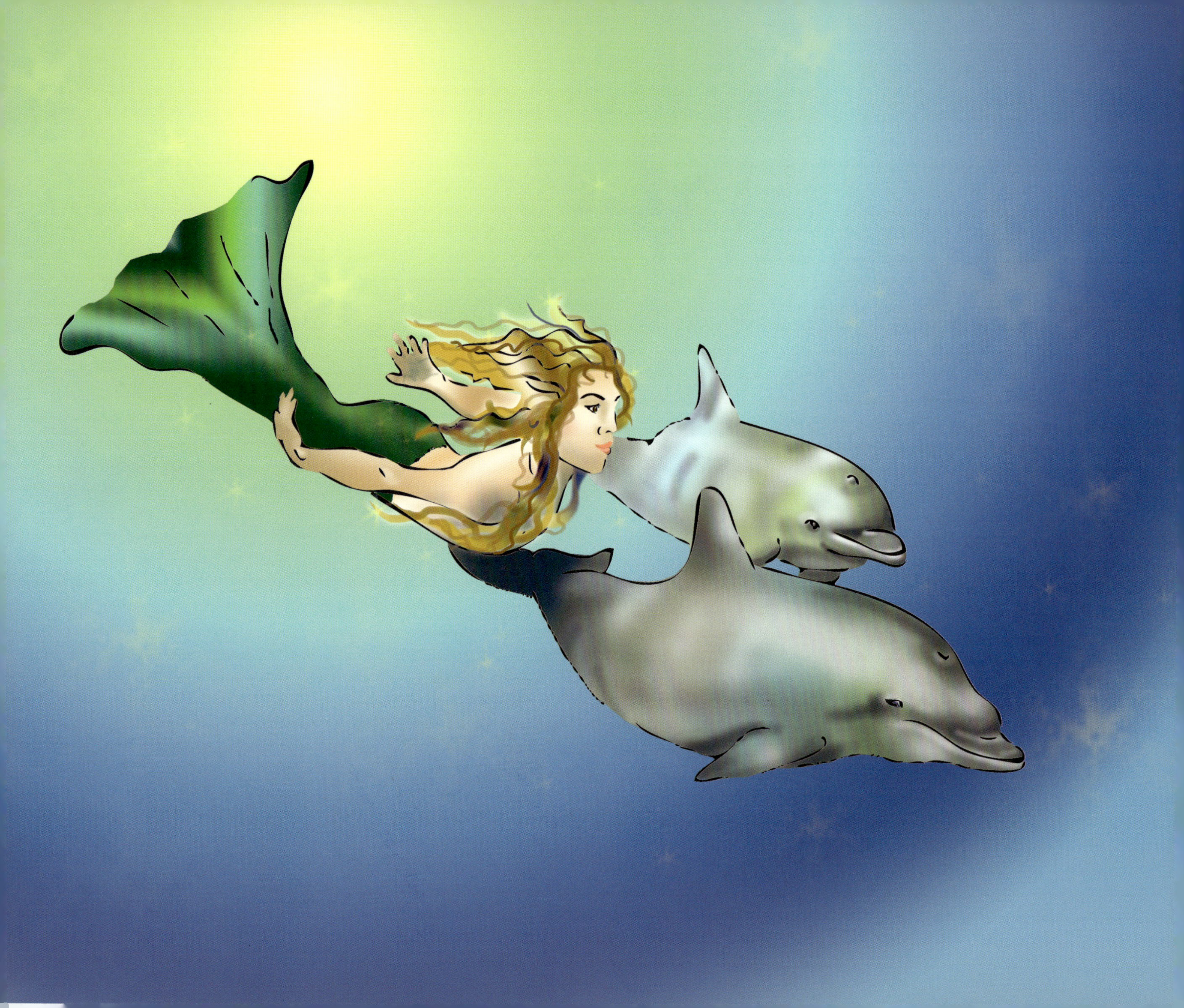

Just like other mermaids, Adaline was charged with learning about her world and how to protect the creatures under her care. With her mer-parents, mer-brother Dylan and dolphin friends, Adaline traveled the breadth and depth of the waters off the Emerald Coast.

She saw red snapper flashing in the sun along the clear aqua waters of Destin. Another calm day allowed flying through water on the wings of manta rays, from Seaside to Panama City.

When the deeper waters turned cold or rough, Adaline's mer-parents brought her to the calmer waters in and around St Joseph Bay. Those days she spent among the sandbars, carefully restoring sand dollars and starfish to their rightful place in the white sands. And on occasion, when she lingered overlong (perhaps a little on purpose) Adaline watched the young human girl and her dog.

One day, while happily enjoying the surface sun, floating close to shore, Adaline heard a woman's voice calling "Suzanne!" Startled, Adaline rose in the gentle surf, sitting on the sandy bottom. Having drifted much closer than intended, she was only waist deep in water, yards from shore. Arrested by the sight of the beach girl staring straight into her eyes, Adaline took several moments to become aware of her dolphin escort loudly calling her back in to deeper waters.

Adaline quickly ducked beneath the water's surface, shyly smiling, having found the name of her land-bound friend. And she thought:

"I wonder what my life would be, if I was Suzanne and she was me. Would she like the cool waters and shimmering light, swimming with dolphins and making a sea bed at night?"

Learning about the world around her, and its history, kept Suzanne very busy. There were field trips to take, books to study and tests to take. Next to spending time at the beach, Suzanne's favorite thing to do was traveling inland to see cousins and visit new places.

She toured the caves of Marianna with her cousin Rachel, fascinated by the stalagmites and stalactites. The trip to Wakulla with her parents and brothers Sam and Evan was exciting, finding manatees swimming in the springs. But then Suzanne was touched with sadness, seeing the marks and scars on the manatee backs, made by propellers from boats going too fast in the waterways, hurting the manatees before they could move away at their slower pace.

Suzanne's favorite place was found on a weekend trip to the state capital, Tallahassee. Happening upon a majestic wooden gateway, they found Mission San Luis, the original settlement of Spaniards, Franciscans and Apalachee Indians, discovered and restored by dedicated archeologists. It was the first of its kind, the three very different peoples living together in cooperation and community. Standing in the domed council house of the Indians, Suzanne felt the power of history and a deep respect for those settlers of yesteryear.

Resting from the heat under a hundreds year old live oak tree, gazing at the fort and church lovingly recreated from history, Suzanne recalled her previous afternoon.

Having lingered too long on the beach she knew she was running late. Taking a last glance out at the gulf before heading home to pack, she heard what sounded like calls coming from near the sandbar. She looked closer, startled to see the young mermaid floating close to shore. As she heard the inevitable call of her mother, "Suzanne, time to get yourself home!" she kept staring at the mermaid, delighted when she had moved to sit up. Looking directly into each other's eyes, a bond was formed. Becoming once again aware of the calling dolphins, Suzanne had heard a repeating chorus, "Adaline, swim home!" Could dolphins talk? As she wondered about this new development her mother once again had called her name, prompting her to turn for home, when she saw the young mermaid slipping back into deeper water. With a smile on her face, she had walked the path between the dunes, with the name of her mermaid friend in her mind and in her heart.

Once again in the present, with her back against the tree and her elbows resting on her knees, Suzanne thought:

"I wonder what my life would be if I was Adaline and she was me? Would she like the still forests or sounds of city life, traveling from place to place by car, running through fields or napping in dappled light?

As she continued to grow in mind and body Adaline the mermaid began asking more questions of others and herself. While some mer-friends were drawn to deeper waters, she preferred the coastal shallows. A few mermaids she knew cared only for having fun, but Adaline knew much needed to be done to nurture and protect their world.

Word had come that human man was more and more interested in the hidden treasures of gulf and sea. It was a point of discussion and some debate among Adaline's mer-parents and others.

And all this time she kept watch on Suzanne, fascinated by the changes. Some days she was the happy and carefree girl running the beach, on others she was in a quiet, thoughtful mood, looking troubled as she sat in strange garb upon her dune. Adaline had seen herself reflected in those varying moods, so she found herself wondering…

"Some may say not to worry, others seem to question everything. I find myself feeling too much -- what do I do with this life I've been given? What is my role, my gift, my purpose? Just to have fun, or is there a deeper answer?... I wonder if Suzanne wonders too?"

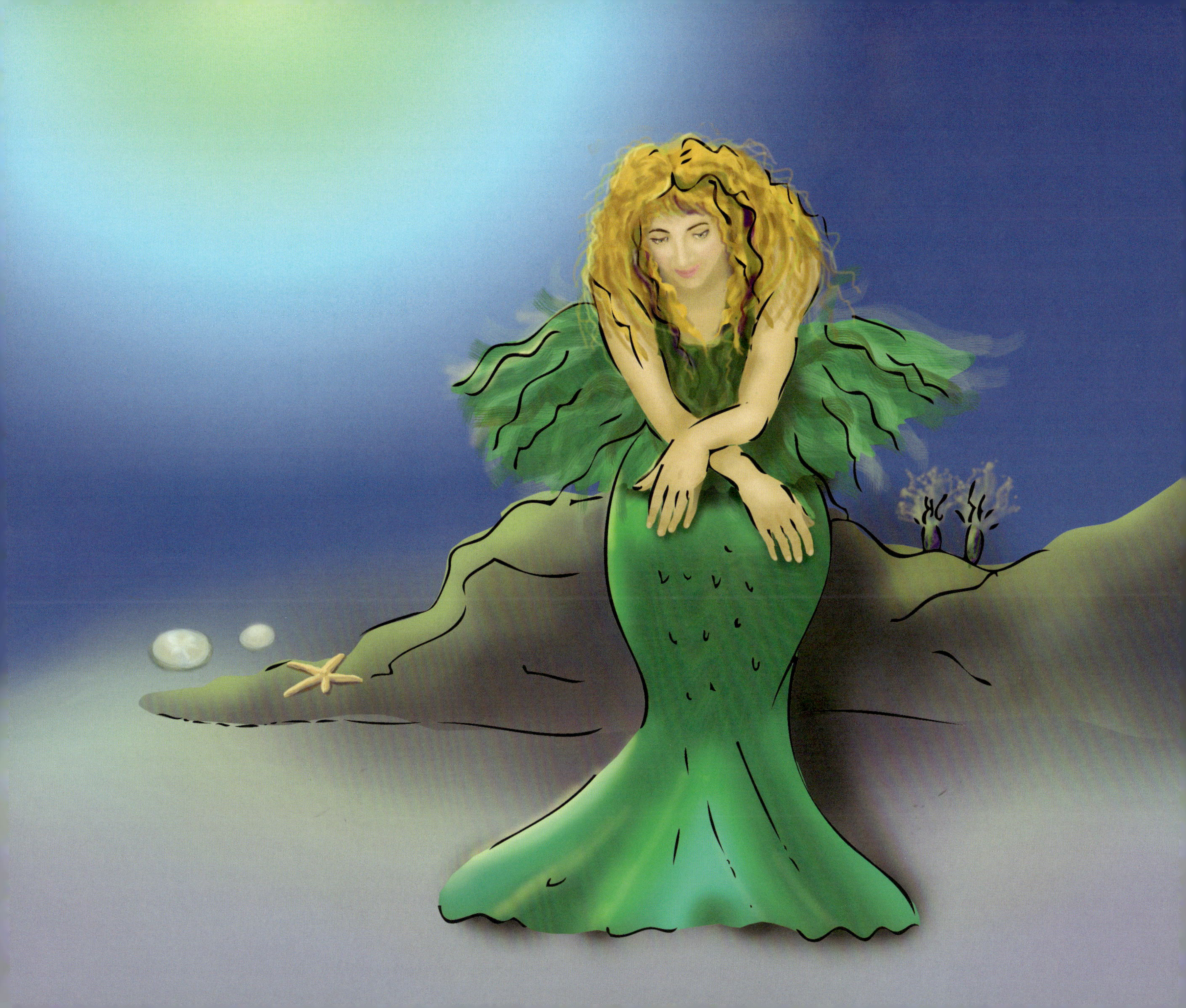

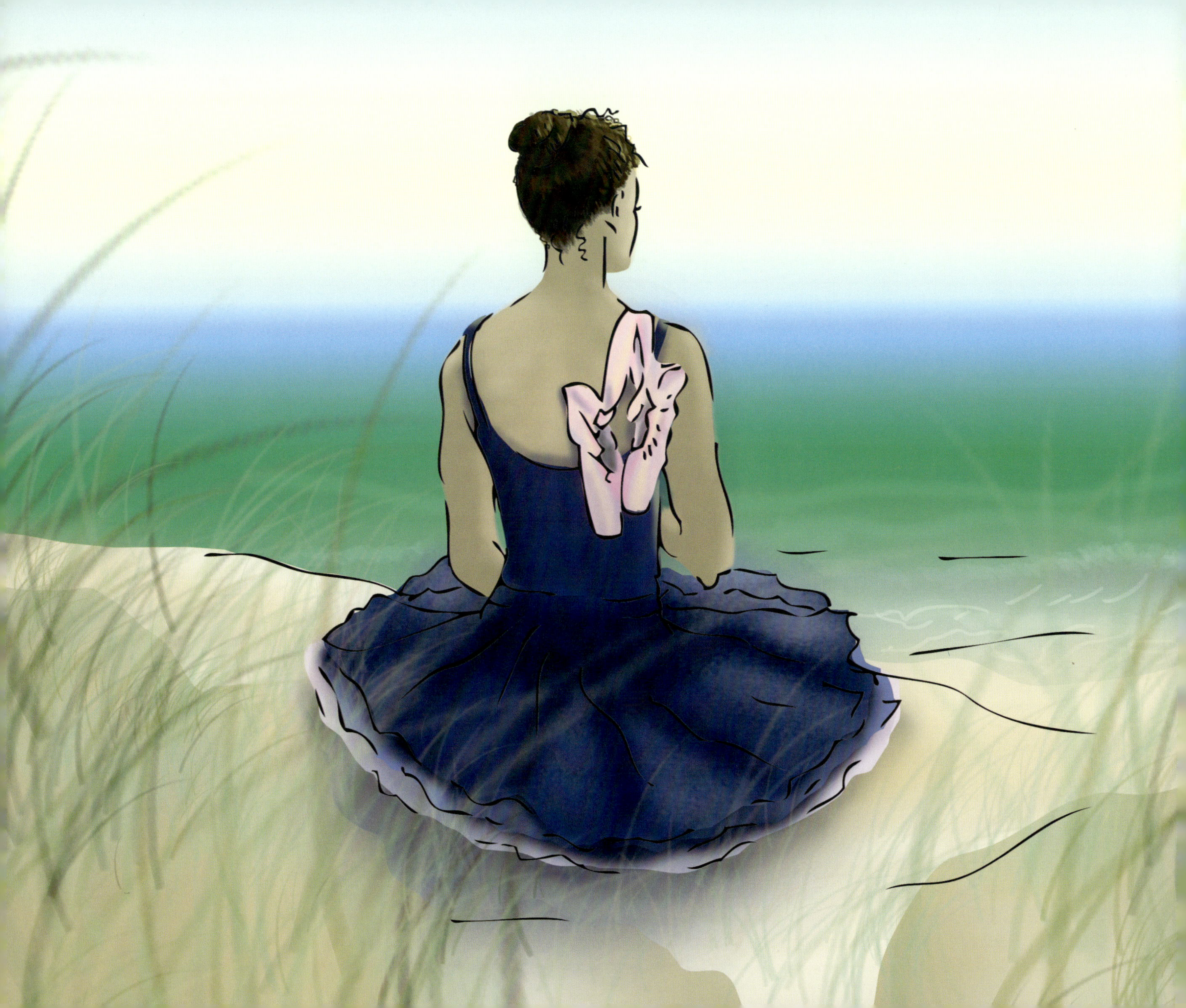

Some days were so easy, others more difficult as Suzanne continued to mature.

She had friends interested only in the popular trends of TV and the internet, while others cared even less about doing good deeds.

Just today Suzanne had returned from dance class to sit upon her favorite dune, thinking of the changing world around her. Of late, she knew there was much discussion among her family about what different people in their circle of friends thought. Should there be more growth and more building? Would less growth mean fewer choices or just different ones in the future?

Suzanne had many questions of her own in her head and heart – so many she was unsure where to start. So she sat in her ballet garb and wondered…

> *"Will I stay or will I go when it comes time to learn more? What talent is inside me? I know it's there, I feel it wanting to burst free and I know that my path is not yet clear enough to see. I just know the answer is somewhere close! … I wonder if Adaline feels this way too?"*

As the moon cycled twelve more times Adaline's full mermaid colors showed in her hair and tail. Admiring her emerald highlights in the filtered light she knew a crossroads was upon her. The small hope that had grown and grown inside her heart had her seeking her mer-parents for counsel.

"Is this hope I have my true gift in life?" Adaline asked.

With their wise and quiet smiles her mer-parents confirmed, "Yes, you are drawn to the shore for a reason. Humans need reminding of certain things and not all will be as special as Suzanne." Seeing their daughter's surprise they continued "Yes, we knew the two of you watched each other. It was meant to be, for she comes from a lineage long in wisdom and caring. Suzanne is our best hope on land for the future of our waters and the creatures we are charged to protect. And there are others like her for you to reach as well. Go, share your gift with her and those others so they may remain strong and inspired."

Swimming to shore, for the first time in her life Adaline emerged fully from the gulf, coming to rest just beyond water's edge beginning her patient wait.

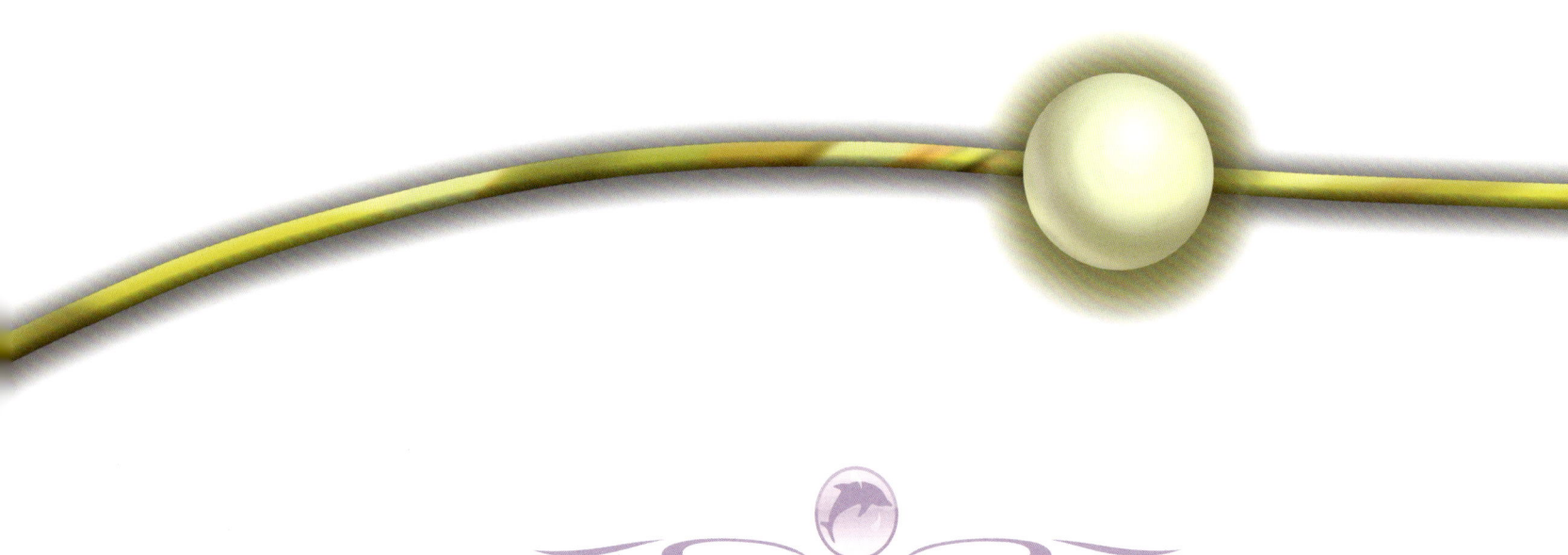

Suzanne was filled with dreams and fears. She knew in her heart what was meant to be, but leaving family and home caused her to question her plans and ideas.

Seeking her grandmother's advice she sat facing the one she would miss beyond compare. Her courage faltered, tears rose and halted the questions needing to be asked. Watching this struggle, her grandmother reached out and laid her right hand upon Suzanne's shoulder, holding in her left the gifted pearl, now a necklace crafted on a cord of gold. "Take this pearl and wear it always. It is a reminder of the things you hold dear, and moments yet to be. Suzanne, you were given a special friend in Adaline the mermaid."

Seeing her granddaughter's startled expression she smiled and continued "Yes, I know that you have watched each other through the years, as was meant to be. And I have proudly witnessed the two of you become beautiful young women, strong of heart and pure with intent. Just as Adaline knows her purpose, so do you. Go now, walk your beach and your questions will be answered. And if at any time you doubt your family's love, touch this pearl and be reminded you have our support and faith in your choices."

Feeling lighter of heart but still uncertain Suzanne took the well worn path between the dunes. With thoughts bumping against each other in her mind and questions pushing against her heart, she strolled the beach thinking of her grandmother's words.

These past few years had been difficult for her family and neighbors. The threat of an oil spill in the Gulf, then a later hurricane, had cut deeply into the tourism that helped support their area of the Emerald Coast.

Slowing her steps when she caught movement ahead, Suzanne was stunned to see Adaline the mermaid out of the water, reclining on shore. In all the years, she had only caught glimpses of the ever changing face and form. Mesmerized by the glimmer of setting sun on the emerald tail, Suzanne wondered if she was imagining this vision.

At that moment, Adaline sat upright, sweeping her tail and long tresses aside. Looking directly into the welcoming hazel eyes of the mermaid, Suzanne took a step forward to say,

"I did not know until this moment how blessed I am to have you as my sister. My choice is made. I will go away to learn, to tell the world through words how important it is we protect these waters. Do you understand?"

Adaline's right hand came to rest near the single pearl on a golden cord she wore around her throat. Raising her left hand, she pointed to Suzanne's matching pearl necklace. Bringing her mermaid hands together over her heart, Adaline used her new found voice to reply,

"Sisters, forever."

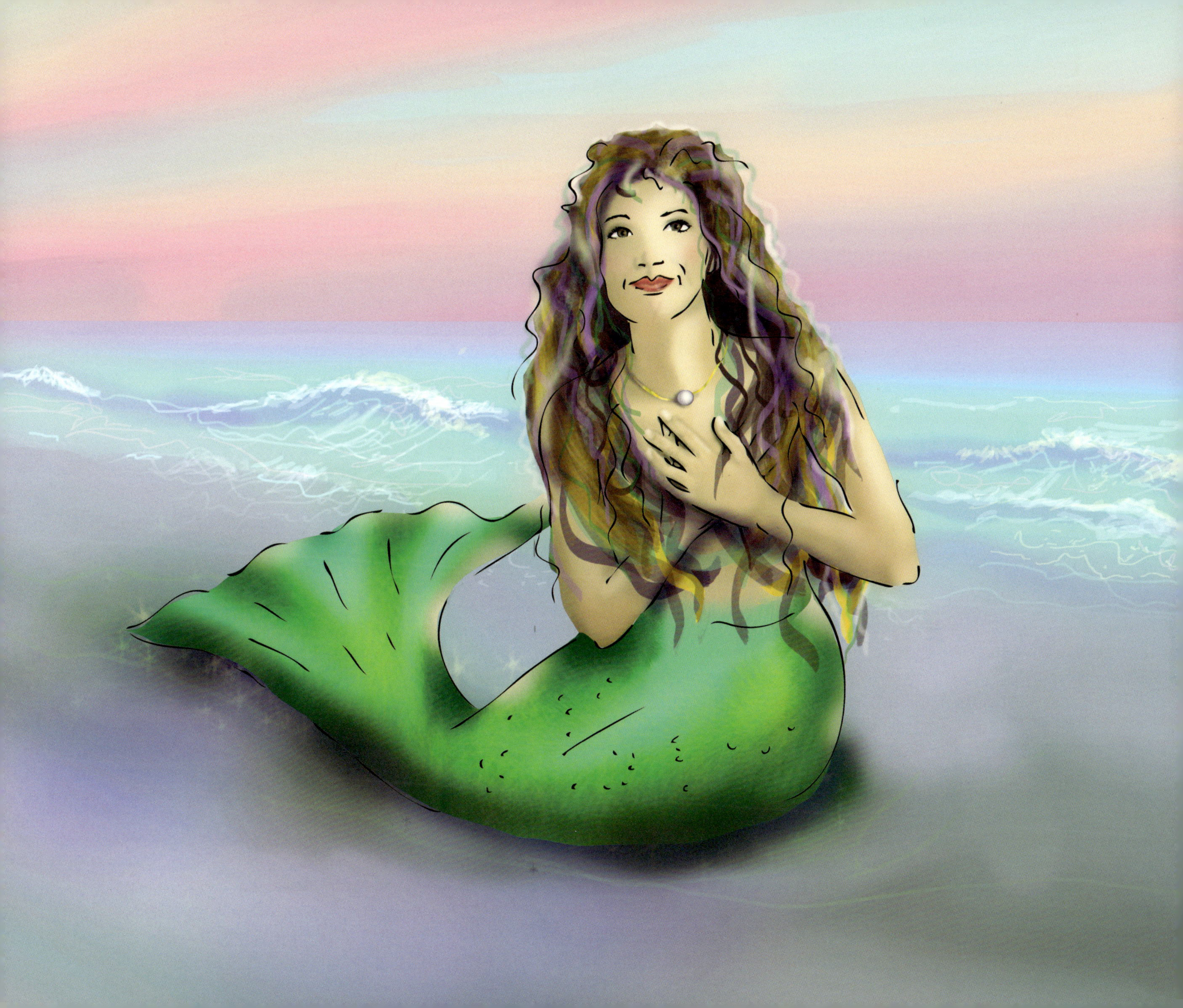

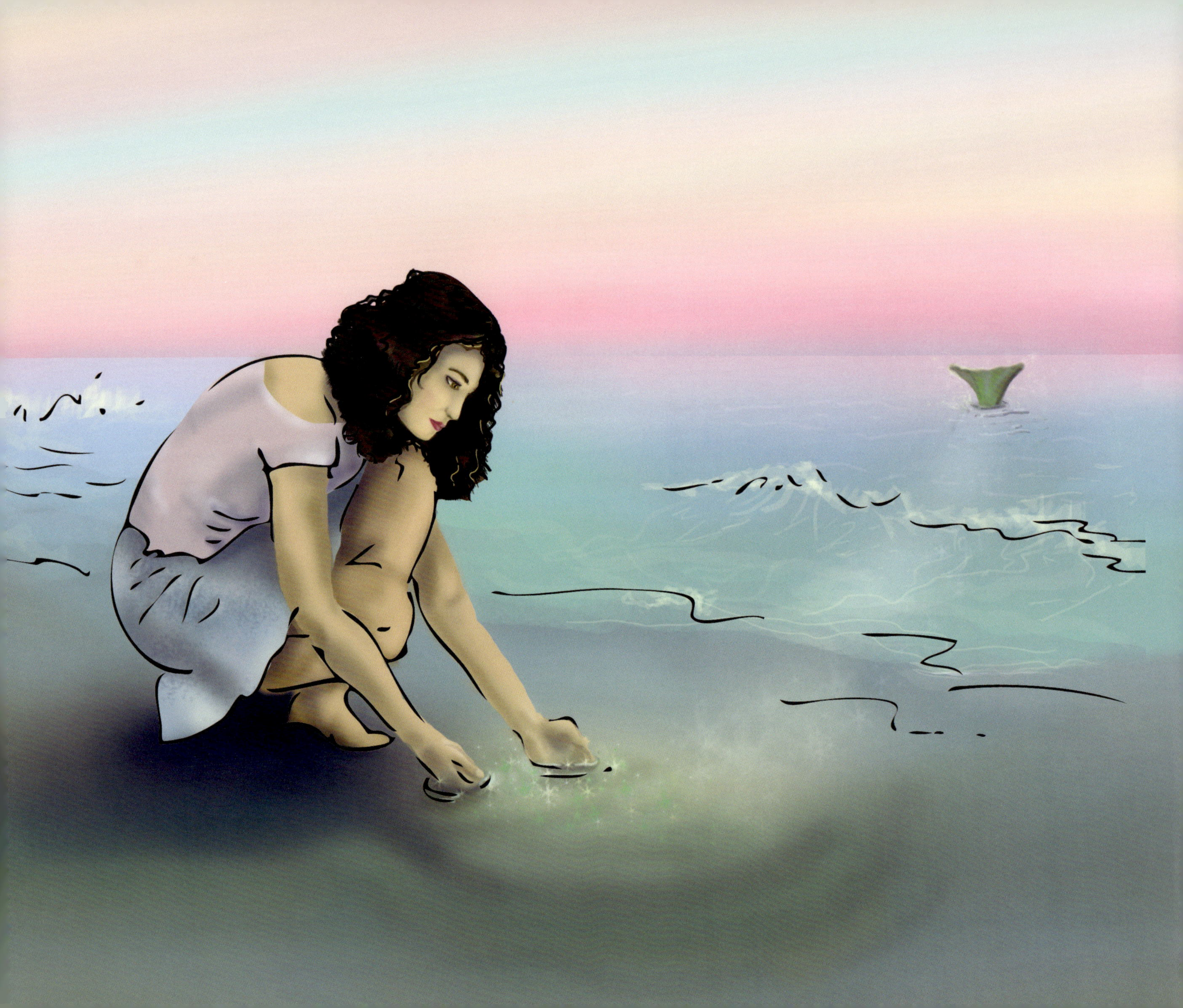

With a joyful smile Adaline stretched toward water's edge, slipping into the gentle surf. In the lowering sunset light she sprang from the water, showering droplets in the air, diving back into an oncoming wave.

Laughing at her sister's antics, Suzanne looked down, to the place Adaline had been resting. Moving closer she saw the sparkling sand. Now she understood the mermaid's special gift, to leave behind a bit of her magic, spreading goodness and hope in the world.

With a final surfacing, Adaline laughed with joy, knowing they were not forever parted. For Suzanne, as she began her walk back home, she felt such hope, such love and sense of rightness she knew her chosen path was true. And both Adaline the mermaid and Susanne the beach girl knew they were never truly parted, even as they each started on their own next adventure.

The End...

until our next Mermaid Sand story...

Where the Story Begins....

I grew up along the Gulf Coast, coming from a family with generations having made their living from the water. There were always stories about storms and beach outings, bonfires and strange sea creatures.

My father sailed the oceans for over 40 years in the Merchant Marine and had his own stories to tell of exotic locales and mesmerizing sights from the bow of ships. My mother was a coastal woman through and through, having had a father who was an oyster-man and herself having worked in the crab picking houses and being a champion oyster shucker. Each of them passed their respect of the water and all its creatures to their children.

One night as a grown women home on a visit, my mother and father gave me a gift, their belief in the Secret of Mermaid Sand.

All the best, Marjorie

A Secret About Mermaids

Have you ever wandered the beach or an edge of a lake and seen a slight indentation in the sand? Something with a little sparkle that for some reason lifted your spirits?

Every generation passes down its knowledge to the next and this is what my coast-dwelling parents gave to me -- the secret of Mermaid Sand.

These elusive and captivating beings known as mermaids dwell just out of sight, being both shy and cautious of all creatures that do not swim naturally within the waters. But the open air, sun, rain and moonlight are a source of wonder to mermaids and they are drawn to resting along the shores to absorb nature's bounty.

If you have ever caught a movement just on the edge of your vision, or seen a sparkling bright reflection along the water's edge, you have seen a mermaid escaping back into her underwater world.

When you come upon the mermaids' resting place you'll find the secret of Mermaid Sand -- little sparkles of magic and wonder she left behind as a reminder that good things are everywhere in this world.

MermaidSand.com

Now I Wish Upon A Pearl
Glossary of Interesting Facts and Findings along the Emerald Coast

Adaline - Word name meaning "noble." Adaline is a mermaid born and raised off Florida's Emerald Coast, mainly around the Mexico Beach area. As she matures she catches glimpses of the human girl Suzanne, until they meet as young women, each coming to find their true gift in life.

Apalachicola - \a-pə-la-chi-kō-lə\ From the Apalachicola tribe and is a combination of Hitchiti Indian words "apalahchi," meaning "on the other side," and "okli," meaning "people". Many inhabitants of Apalachicola choose to translate the name of their town as "land of the friendly people." Apalachicola is located in the northwest part of the state, on Apalachicola Bay and at the mouth of the Apalachicola River. Apalachicola is the home port for a variety of seafood workers, including oyster harvesters and shrimpers. More than 90% of Florida's oyster production is harvested from Apalachicola Bay http://www.apalachicolabay.org/ or http://historicapalachicola.info/

Destin - Located on Florida's Emerald Coast, Destin is known for its white beaches and emerald green waters. Originating as a small fishing village, it is now a popular tourist destination. The city is located on a peninsula separating the Gulf of Mexico from Choctawhatchee Bay. The sand on Destin's beaches is some of the whitest in the world, often referred to as sugar sand. http://www.destin.com/

Dolphins - Dolphins are marine mammals that are closely related to whales and porpoises. There are almost forty species of dolphin. They are found worldwide, mostly in the shallower seas of the continental shelves. Dolphins are among the most intelligent animals, and their friendly appearance and playful attitude make them perfect companions and protectors of mermaids.

cont...

Dylan – Welsh origin. In Welsh mythology Dylan was a god of the sea and the son of Gwyddion and Arianrhod. Dylan is the mer-brother to Adaline, the Emerald Coast Mermaid.

Emerald Coast - Florida's Emerald Coast features miles of pristine white-sand beaches stretching along the Gulf of Mexico. This sand, made up of pure Appalachian quartz, remains remarkably cool even in the heat of summer, and gives the waters their trademark emerald-green color by reflecting sunlight back up through the surf.

Evan – Brother of Suzanne. Welsh masculine name, derived from "Iefan", a Welsh form of John; the name John is derived from the ancient Hebrew name Yəhô⊚ānān, which means "God Is Gracious". Evan is also a Celtic name meaning "Young Warrior".

Gulf Oil Spill – The most recent oil spill in the Gulf of Mexico which flowed for three months in 2010 was the largest accidental marine oil spill in the history of the petroleum industry. The spill stemmed from a sea-floor oil gusher that resulted from the April 20, 2010, explosion of Deepwater Horizon. On July 15, 2010, the leak was stopped by capping the gushing wellhead, after it had released about 4.9 million barrels of crude oil. The spill caused extensive damage to marine and wildlife habitats and to the Gulf's fishing and tourism industries.

Manatee – A large, fully aquatic, mostly herbivorous marine mammals sometimes known as sea cows. They measure up to 13 feet long, weigh as much as 1,300 pounds and have paddle-like flippers. At any given time, a manatee typically has no more than six teeth in each jaw of its mouth. Uniquely among mammals, these teeth are continuously replaced throughout life, with new teeth growing at the rear as older teeth fall out from farther forward in the mouth. Half a manatee's day is spent sleeping in the water, surfacing for air regularly at intervals no greater than 20 minutes. Manatees spend most of the rest of the time grazing in shallow waters at depths of 3–6 ft. The manatee has been known to live up to 60 years.

Manta ray – The manta ray is the largest species of the rays, growing up to more than 25 ft across, with a weight of 2,900 pounds. It ranges throughout tropical waters of the world, typically around coral reefs. Mantas feed on plankton, fish larvae and the like, filtered from the water passing through their mouths and out of their gills as they swim. They are exceptionally graceful swimmers and appear to fly through the water on their large wings. Female mantas give birth to live young with the average litter size of two pups.

Marianna Caves - Florida Caverns State Park is located in the Florida Panhandle near Marianna. It is home to the only air-filled caves accessible to visitors. The caverns were formed over time as water seeped into and dissolved rock, forming dazzling formations of limestone stalactites, stalagmites, soda straws, flowstones and draperies. http://www.floridastateparks.org/floridacaverns/

Mexico Beach – Where Suzanne and her family live and where Adaline comes to the shallow waters to play and rest. Mexico Beach is located between Port St. Joe and Panama City and is known for white sand beaches and calm, clear waters protected by Cape San Blas. http://mexico-beach.com/

Mission San Luis – Located in Tallahassee, Florida, Mission San Luis transports you back in time to a community where Apalachee Indians and newcomers from Spain lived in close proximity, drawn together by religion as well as military and economic purpose. http://www.missionsanluis.org/

Panama City – Panama City Beach Florida offers 27 miles of white sand beaches, emerald green waters and enjoyment in, on or under the water. Panama City Beach claims to be the "Seafood Capital of the World".

Port St. Joe - Port St. Joe is located within the Florida Panhandle along the Emerald Coast. Port St. Joe almost became the capital of Florida in the 19th Century. The state constitution was ratified there in 1838 and there is a museum and monument commemorating this event.
http://www.visitgulf.com/port-st-joe

cont...

Rachel – Word origin meaning "one of purity." Cousin of Suzanne that lives inland and took a day trip together to the Marianna caves.

Red Snapper – The red snapper is a fish found in the Gulf of Mexico and the southeastern Atlantic coast of the United States. The red snapper commonly inhabits waters thirty to two hundred feet deep, but some are reported to be caught at three hundred feet deep. Coloration of the red snapper is light red, with more intense pigment on the back. An adult snapper can live for more than 50 years and weigh 50 pounds. Snappers are gregarious and will form large schools around wrecks and reefs making them a fun friend of mermaids.

Sam – Word origin meaning "sun child" or "bright sun." Brother of Suzanne

Sand Dollar - Sand dollars live on top of or just beneath the surface of sandy or muddy sea floors. On the ocean bottom, sand dollars are frequently found together.

Sandbar – Long, relatively narrow bands of sand under shallow surf running parallel to shore. Sandbars form where waves are breaking, because the breaking waves set up a shoreward current with a returning counter-current along the bottom. Sand carried by the offshore moving bottom current is deposited where the current reaches the wave break. Adaline enjoys playing and resting just inside the sandbars, often checking on her sand dollar friends.

Seaside – Located between Panama City and Destin it is a community begun in 1979 to create an old-fashioned beach town of wood-framed cottages in the Florida Panhandle building tradition.

Stalactites – Stalactites are formed by calcium carbonate and other minerals. An average growth rate is 0.0051 inches a year. Every stalactite begins with a single mineral-laden drop of water. When the drop falls, it deposits the thinnest ring of calcite. Each subsequent drop that forms and falls deposits another calcite ring.

Stalagmites – A stalagmite rises from the floor of a limestone cave such as Marianna cave due to the dripping of minerals and calcium carbonate. Stalagmites should not be touched, since they can often break and skin oils can alter the surface affecting the growth of the formation.

Starfish – Starfish occur across a broad depth range from tidal pools to the deep sea. Starfish are among the most familiar of marine animals and possess a number of widely known traits, such as re-growing a part of their body when broken off by accident. Starfish come in many shapes and sizes and they occur in all of the Earth's oceans.

Tallahassee – \ta-lə-ha-sē\ Tallahassee is the capital of the state of Florida and is located inland from the Gulf of Mexico approximately 25 miles. It is home to Florida State University and Florida A&M University as well as many interesting sites to see. Mission San Luis gives a glimpse of history, Tallahassee Museum bring nature within reach – plan your stay to be a full one! www.tallahassee.com/livinghere http://www.visittallahassee.com/

Wakulla Springs - Wakulla Spring is classified as a first magnitude spring and is the longest and deepest known submerged freshwater cave system in the world. Flow rate of the spring is 200-300 million US gallons of water a day. The spring forms the Wakulla River which flows 9 miles to the southeast where it joins the St. Mark's River. After a short 5 miles the St. Mark's empties into the Gulf of Mexico at Apalachee Bay. Suzanne and her family visit Wakulla Springs to see the Manatee during the summer. http://www.floridastateparks.org/wakullasprings/

Find out more at: www.MermaidSand.com!

facebook.com/mermaidsand

twitter: MermaidSand

Adaline, the Emerald Coast Mermaid

Now I Wish Upon a Pearl
Capture the moment of wonder with Adaline wishing upon her magical pearl.

Swimming with Dolphins
Feel the cool Gulf water and the exhilaration of swimming freely with Adaline and her dolphin friends.

Sisters Forever
Relive the heart touching moment when Adaline and Suzanne realize their true gifts in life.

Available as ready to frame art prints or specialty note cards
Art prints: 11" x 14"
Note cards* too!

Log on to **www.MermaidSand.com** to place your order, call **850.363.2215 9-5 EST**

See shipping charges on order form, thanks!

*note cards come with excerpt from book on the back, blank on the inside and each is accompanied by a perfectly sized, bright envelope - fun and functional!

Mermaid Sand™ Jewelry

$12 each or all 3 for $30 (great gift item)

Choose from a playful dolphin, colorful fish or sophisticated vial - these intricate glass designs come hand filled with Mermaid Sand™

Ready to wear on beautifully colored ribbon and suede necklaces.

Sign up for our Mermaid Tails Newsletter and get VIP advance notices on upcoming events and new Mermaids
Coming soon, Aurora, the Alaskan Mermaid and the LIMITED EDITION Scottish Mermaid (name held till release date)

Adaline, The Emerald Coast Mermaid Sand

The cork stoppered glass bottle contains magical Mermaid Sand™ honored with the colors of Adaline, and has *hidden treasures within.* Nestled in a shimmering emerald organza bag, Adaline's Mermaid Sand™ is accompanied by an 8 x 11" rolled *parchment containing excerpts* of the quotes from this book, **Now I Wish Upon a Pearl**.

Begin your collection with the original Mermaid Sand Secret bottle and scroll, then continue the journey with Adaline's treasure filled bottle.

Hidden Treasures in Adaline, The Emerald Coast Mermaid Sand

In each hand filled bottle of Adaline Mermaid Sand you will find a genuine Swarovski crystal in glittering emerald facets, a fresh water pearl to honor the pearl gifts of Adaline and Suzanne and a specially selected part of an Emerald Coast shell. And of course, that bit of mermaid magic that sparkles and shines, reminding us all that we each have special talents to share and that there is goodness and hope everywhere in this world.

Yes! I would like these Mermaid Sand treasures.

___ x $15 Adaline Treasures and Letter

___ x $20 Now I Wish Upon A Pearl Book (hardcover)

___ x $15 Art print Now I Wish Upon A Pearl

___ x $15 Art print Swimming with Dolphins

___ x $15 Art print Sisters Forever

___ x $35 Set of all 3 art prints

Total from both columns $_____

___ x $3 notecard _____ (indicate choice)

___ x $15 for set of 6 notecards

Notecard price includes envelopes

___ x $12 Mermaid Sand filled dolphin necklace

___ x $12 Mermaid Sand filled glittering fish necklace

___ x $12 Mermaid Sand filled modern vial

___ x $30 for ALL 3 Mermaid Sand filled necklaces

+Plus $8 shipping for orders under $36, $16 shipping for orders totalling $36 and above (only necklaces? $5 shipping)

Name_____ e-mail _____ Phone_____

Address _____ State_____ Zip_____

Total amount (including shipping) $_____ Check enclosed _____ Money Order_____

Go to MermaidSand.com to order online or copy this form and mail to: Mermaid Sand ™, 6551 Crooked Creek Rd, Tallahassee, FL 32311 or email: Marjorie@MermaidSand.com

A Map of Forida's Emerald Coast